Karen's Grandmothers

**Here are some other books
about Karen
that you might enjoy:**

Little Sister

Karen's Grandmothers

Ann M. Martin

Illustrations by Susan Tang

A
LITTLE APPLE
PAPERBACK

SCHOLASTIC INC.
New York Toronto London Auckland Sydney

ISBN 0-590-43651-1

12 11 10 9 8 7 6   3 4 5/9

Printed in the U.S.A.   28

First Scholastic printing, August 1990

This book is for
Bethany Buck,
who helps make Karen come alive

Adopt-a-Grandparent

It was hot, hot, hot in Ms. Colman's classroom.

I waited until she turned her back. Then I whispered to Ricky Torres, "Why do we have to start school in September? Why couldn't we start in October, when it is cooler?"

"Because," Ricky replied, glancing at Ms. Colman, "we would have to go to school in July to make up for it."

"Oh," I said. "Then I wish we could have an air conditioner in our classroom."

1

Ricky grinned at me. I like Ricky and he likes me.

Who am I? I am Karen Brewer. I am seven years old. I go to Stoneybrook Academy with Hannie Papadakis and Nancy Dawes. They are my very best friends. We call ourselves the Three Musketeers. We are all in Ms. Colman's second-grade class. I wear glasses and have freckles. Once, I broke my wrist.

It was the end of the day. Everyone in my room was tired. I could tell. But soon we perked up. That was because Ms. Colman said, "Class, I have a special announcement to make."

Ms. Colman's special announcements usually really are pretty special. My friends and I like Ms. Colman. She is full of surprises, and she never yells.

"How many of you," began Ms. Colman, "have heard of the Adopt-a-Grandparent program?"

I looked around the room. Not a single hand was raised.

2

"Okay," said Ms. Colman, "how many of you know what Stoneybrook Manor is?"

My hand shot up.

"Karen?" said Ms. Colman.

"Stoneybrook Manor is a place in town where old people live when they can't take care of themselves very well anymore."

"That's right," said Ms. Colman. "And our class has been given a special honor. We've been chosen to 'adopt' some of the people there. Anyone who is interested will be assigned to a resident. You'll visit your new 'grandparent' twice a week after school. It will mean a lot to the people there. Some of them don't have any visitors at all. They are very lonely. Who would like to adopt a grandparent?"

I raised my hand right away. (So did Ricky and Hannie and several other kids, but not Nancy.) Here's the thing. My parents are divorced. Then they each got married again. So I have *four* grandmothers — two regular ones, and two stepgrandmothers. If I adopted a fifth grandma, I would

3

break the grandmother record for good!

"If you would like to talk about this with your friends," said Ms. Colman, "I will give you ten minutes to do that. You may leave your seats."

I jumped up and ran to the back of the classroom to Hannie and Nancy. (We used to sit in the back row together, but Ms. Colman moved me to the front row when I got my glasses.)

4

"Nancy," I said, "don't you want to adopt a grandmother or grandfather? You don't have any of your own."

"Nope," replied Nancy.

"But grandparents are great," I told her. "They like to give stuff to kids. Adopting a grandparent will be fun. Besides, some of the people in the home are really lonely. They need us."

"No," said Nancy flatly.

"Well, I want an adopted grandparent," said Hannie.

"Good," I replied. "So does Ricky. So do a bunch of other kids."

When the ten minutes were up, Ms. Colman asked us to sit down again. Then she handed out permission slips to the kids who wanted to adopt grandparents. "A bus will take you to the manor and then pick you up each time you visit," she told us.

BRINNNNG! rang the bell.

School was over.

I could not wait to tell Mommy that soon I might have *five* grandmas.

Karen's Four Grandmas

My four grandmothers are named Grandma, Granny, Nannie, and Neena. That can be pretty confusing! Grandma and Neena are my regular grandmothers. Granny and Nannie are my stepgrandmothers. Are you still confused? Okay, I'll try to explain better.

When Mommy got married again, she married a man named Seth. Seth is my stepfather. And Granny is Seth's mother. She lives on a farm in the state of Nebraska, which is far, far away.

When Daddy got married again, he married a woman named Elizabeth. Elizabeth is my stepmother. And Nannie is her mother. She lives with Elizabeth and Daddy.

It is a good thing that Daddy has a big house (it is really a mansion) because a lot of other people live in it besides Daddy, Elizabeth, and Nannie. First of all, Elizabeth has four children. They are: Charlie and Sam, who are in high school (Sam is a big tease); Kristy, who is thirteen and the president of a business called the Baby-sitters Club (she is also one of my most favorite people — I love having Kristy for *my* baby-sitter!); and David Michael, who is seven like I am. He's in second grade, too, but we go to different schools. Then there is Emily Michelle. Daddy and Elizabeth adopted her. She came from a country called Vietnam. Emily is only two and a half. I named my rat after her. Also at the big house are two pets: One is Shannon, David Michael's puppy. The other is Boo-Boo, Daddy's fat, old, mean cat.

Mommy and Seth have a much smaller house. That is because not so many people live there. There are Mommy and Seth. Oh, and Andrew and me, of course. Andrew is my little brother. He's four, going on five. Plus, there are three pets at the little house: Emily Junior, my rat; and Rocky and Midgie, Seth's cat and dog.

Guess what. Mommy and Daddy both live in Stoneybrook, Connecticut. This is handy for Andrew and me because it means we can spend time with both Mommy and Daddy. Mostly, we live at Mommy's house. But every other weekend and for two weeks each summer we live at Daddy's. Since we go back and forth so much, I call my brother and me the two-twos. I am Karen Two-Two, and Andrew is Andrew Two-Two. I got the name from a book Ms. Colman read to our class. It is called *Jacob Two-Two Meets the Hooded Fang*. Two-Two is a good name for us because we have two of so many things. We have two families and two houses. I have two unicorn shirts, one at each house.

I have two bicycles, one at each house. (So does Andrew.) I have two stuffed cats, one at each house. Moosie stays at the big house, Goosie stays at the little house. I even have two best friends. Nancy lives next door to the little house, and Hannie lives across the street from the big house. Being a two-two isn't always easy, though. I don't have two of *every*thing, of course. For instance, I only have one pair of roller skates. And for the longest time, I only had one Tickly, my special blanket. When I kept leaving Tickly behind at one house or the other, I finally had to rip my blanket in half. That way, I could have a piece at each house.

Sometimes being a two-two is fun. Sometimes it is not so much fun.

But I do like having four grandmas. That is gigundo special. And if I could have a fifth, that would be even better. I did not know anybody else with five grandmas.

Nancy's No Grandmas

Nancy Dawes's mother drove Nancy and me home after school. Nancy does not have any brothers or sisters, just her mom and her dad. That is why I wished she would adopt a grandparent. Nancy needs a bigger family.

As soon as Mrs. Dawes had parked her car in the driveway, I unbuckled my seat belt, said, "Thank you!" and ran home.

"Mommy?" I called. "Mommy?" I burst through the front door of the little house.

"Hi, honey!" Mommy replied.

I found Mommy in the kitchen. She was helping Andrew with a project for school. They were using a lot of glue.

I pulled my permission slip out of my backpack. I whisked it in front of Mommy.

"Here," I said. "I am going to adopt a grandparent. If it is a grandmother, then I will have *five* grandmas," I told Mommy proudly. "See? We will go to Stoneybrook Manor two times a week. This is a special

honor for the kids in Ms. Colman's class," I added.

"Two afternoons a week?" said Mommy. "But Karen, you are already very busy. You take art lessons on Wednesdays now, sometimes you meet with your Fun Club, and sometimes you have Krushers practices." (The Krushers are a softball team that my big sister coaches.)

"I know," I said to Mommy. "But I really, really, really want to adopt a grandparent. Especially a grandma."

"Even though you'll be busy two more afternoons each week?" she asked.

"Yes," I said. I nodded my head firmly.

"Okay," said Mommy. She signed my permission slip.

"Oh, thank you!" I cried. I gave Mommy a gigundo kiss on her forehead. Then I said, "I'm going over to Nancy's now!"

"Be home before dinner," called Mommy, as I ran out the door.

"I will!" I called back.

I ran to the Daweses' and found Nancy in her room.

"Mommy signed my permission slip," I announced first thing.

"Good," said Nancy. She flopped on her bed.

"What's wrong?" I asked, sitting next to her.

"I don't know."

"I think you need a grandma or a grandpa," I said.

"No! I do *not* need one!"

"Why? Why won't you go to Stoneybrook Manor?"

Nancy looked embarrassed. "I am afraid of old people," she said after a long time. "I don't have any grandparents." She paused. "Sometimes I wish I did. But most times, I think I would be afraid of them."

"You are not afraid of Nannie," I pointed out. (Nancy has met Nannie at the big house lots of times.)

"Nannie does not seem like an old person," Nancy replied. "She goes bowling.

14

She drives a car. She doesn't even *look* old. I am afraid of *really old* people, and most grandparents are really old."

"Why do old people scare you?" I asked.

Nancy just shrugged.

After awhile I decided to go home. I was not bored . . . I was getting an idea.

Pen-Pal Grandmother

As I walked back to my house, I thought about Nancy and old people. I wanted to show Nancy that "old" does not mean "bad" or "scary." Maybe some old people are scary, but most of them are just regular, except that they have wrinkles and gray or white hair — or no hair at all. And some of them can't walk as fast as younger people. They might even need a wheelchair. But those are not reasons to be afraid of them. Younger people have different colors of hair, too. Sometimes they dye it. And babies can't walk at all!

I wished I could find a grandparent for Nancy. That was my idea — to find a grandparent who would not be scary. Now, who could I get? I went to my room to think. Nannie? No. She was too busy. Maybe one of my other grandmas. After all, I had four, and maybe five. I could certainly share one with a friend.

Then I got one of my best ideas ever. I would write to Granny in Nebraska. Maybe she could be Nancy's pen-pal grandmother! Nancy would never have to see how old Granny looks. And if she got some special mail, she would feel almost like she really did have a grandma.

This was perfect. Nancy could have a grandma and she would not feel afraid.

I ran to my room. I got out a pencil and my stationery. At the top of my stationery it says: XXX Kisses From Karen.

Granny gave it to me.

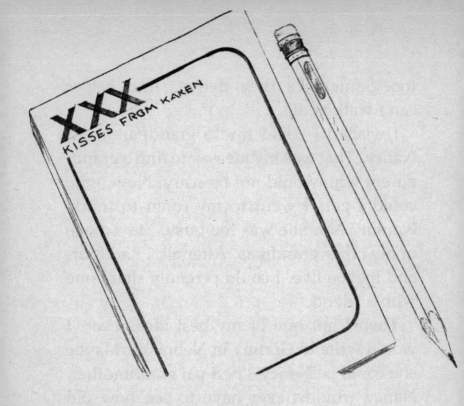

I thought for a long time.
Then I wrote:

Dear Granny

very carefully. Underneath that I wrote:

How are you? Andrew and
I are fine. I really
like this paper.

Finally I got to the point. I told Granny all about Nancy. I told her that she's very nice and that she loves to act. I said maybe she would be an actress one day. Then I added that Nancy does not have any brothers or sisters or any grandmas or grandpas. I said I thought Nancy needed a grandma, even though she was scared of old people. I asked if Granny would like to be her pen-pal grandma. I even made a piece of paper that said:

I WOULD LIKE TO BE A
PEN-PAL GRANDMA

Under that I drew two boxes. Next to one I wrote YES. Next to the other I wrote NO. I hoped that Granny would check the YES box and send the paper back. When I finished my letter, I sealed it up. I mailed it in the box down the street.

Grandma B

It was a big day!

I was so excited I had butterflies in my stomach all during school.

Guess what would happen in the afternoon. Hannie and Ricky and I and some other kids would ride a bus to Stoneybrook Manor. We were going to meet our new grandparents for the first time. We were going to adopt them!

"What do you think our grandparents will be like?" I asked Ricky, as we were finally climbing on the bus.

"Old," he answered.

I giggled. Then I did not feel so nervous.

The bus rolled through town. I felt very proud of myself. I, Karen Brewer, was going to help an old person. And maybe I would set a new grandmother record!

When the bus stopped, I looked at Hannie. We were in the parking lot of Stoneybrook Manor. Soon we would be inside!

Hannie and I stepped off the bus. We held hands. Hannie was nervous.

"Don't be afraid," I whispered to her.

Ms. Colman and two room mothers were with us. They walked us to the front door of the manor.

Two old men were sitting outside in wheelchairs. Blankets were tucked around their knees. One was bald. The other had white hair.

"Look at all the little tots," cackled one.

"Ooh, I'm glad Nancy isn't here," I said to Hannie.

A woman met us at the door. She told us

her name was Mrs. Fellows. Then she led us inside, down a hallway, and into a large room. Sitting in the room were nine people — five women and four men. Three of them were in wheelchairs. They smiled at us. We smiled back.

Somehow, I knew that *every*body was nervous. Even Ms. Colman.

Mrs. Fellows began to speak. "Welcome, Ms. Colman's class," she said. "I know you are eager to meet your new grandparents, so I will read each of your names and the name of your adopted grandparent right away. Then you can have a chance to get acquainted."

Oh, please, please, please let me have another grandmother! I thought.

And then the lady read my name, Karen Brewer, and the name Esther Barnard. *Esther*. That's a woman's name, isn't it?

I looked around the room. A white-haired woman was raising her hand.

She was not sitting in a wheelchair.

I ran to her. "Hi!" I said. "I'm Karen, and you are Esther Barnard. Guess what. You are my fifth grandmother!"

"My goodness," said Esther Barnard.

"Guess what else. I have a brother, three stepbrothers, a stepsister, and an adopted sister. Do you have a family?" I asked.

"Yes, but they live in Chicago," replied Esther Barnard. "I have two daughters and six grandchildren. Four boys and twin girls."

"Twins!" I exclaimed.

"Do you want to see some pictures?" Esther Barnard pulled a package of photos out of her purse. She showed me everyone in her family and told me about them.

Then I told her about the people in my two families, but I did not have any pictures with me. Maybe I should start carrying some.

The hour was over before I knew it. Just as Ms. Colman was saying, "Okay, it's time to go," I turned to Esther Barnard.

"What should I call you?" I asked her.

"How about Grandma B?" she suggested.

I grinned. I like that name. "Perfect!" I said. "And you can call me Karen!"

A Letter for Karen

When I came home from Stoneybrook Manor, I was feeling very happy. I ran inside my house.

"Guess what!" I shouted.

"Indoor voice," Mommy reminded me. She was reading a story to Andrew.

I lowered my voice. "Guess what. I have *five* grandmas now. My new grandma is named Esther Barnard, but I will call her Grandma B."

Mommy smiled. Then she said, "You got some mail today, Karen."

Me?! I got *mail?* Kids almost *never* get mail, except on their birthdays.

"Where is it?" I cried.

"On the kitchen table," said Mommy.

On the table in the kitchen I found a fat envelope. The return address was Nebraska. It must be from Granny! I opened the envelope nice and slowly so I wouldn't rip it. Inside I found the "I would like to be a pen-pal grandma" paper with the "YES" box checked, a letter, and another envelope.

The second envelope said "Nancy Dawes" on the front. Oh, boy!

I looked at my own letter. It said, "Dear Karen, It was so nice to hear from you. Thank you for writing!

"I would love to be your friend's pen-pal grandma. I think you are doing a very nice thing for her. So I am sending her a letter. You can take it to her and explain who it is from."

My idea had worked! I had to get to Nancy's house right away. I picked up Nancy's letter from Granny. That was when I realized how fat it was. Granny had sent Nancy more than just a letter. Hmm. What was it?

There was only one way to find out. I ran the envelope over to Nancy's.

"Guess what," I said to her. Nancy and I sat on her bed.

"What?" asked Nancy.

"You have a grandmother now!" I handed Nancy the envelope.

"I have a grandmother?" Nancy looked quite surprised.

"Yes," I said. I explained what I had done. Then I said, "And here's your first letter from Granny. I — I think she sent you something else, too."

Nancy opened the envelope slowly. She pulled out a letter . . . and a lot of photos of Granny's farm.

I didn't get any photos.

"Wow," said Nancy. "I *like* getting mail." She read her letter. "Gosh," she said when she was done, "your grandmother doesn't sound too old, Karen. She says she feeds the chickens every day. And sometimes she rides a tractor!"

"Will you write back to her?" I asked.

"Well . . . well, sure," replied Nancy. "I guess I have to. But it will be fun." She looked through the photos. "Your grandparents have a lot of animals," she said. "Horses and cows and chickens and even a goat. I guess I should send your grandmother some pictures, too, shouldn't I? I could send her pictures of our house and my room. Too bad we don't have any pets."

After awhile, I went home. I was glad my idea had worked. I knew I had done something nice for both Granny and Nancy. But why hadn't Granny sent *me* any pictures? I could not stop wondering about that.

Oh, well. At least Nancy was happy. She had a grandmother and she was going to send her some pictures.

Maybe I should send Granny some pictures, too. I decided that would be a good idea. And while I was at it, I would take some pictures to show Grandma B. Then I could pull pictures out of my backpack for her.

Grandparents' Day

Two weeks went by. I visited Grandma B four more times. I took pictures of Mommy and Daddy and Andrew and brought them to Stoneybrook Manor to show her. While I was at it, I sent copies of the pictures to Granny in Nebraska.

One day in school, Ms. Colman made another one of her surprise announcements. It was about fifteen minutes before the end of school. Ms. Colman stood up from her desk.

"Class," she said, "I have an announce-

31

ment to make. You may put your books away now so you can listen to me."

There was a little flurry while we put our books in our desks. I wondered what the announcement would be. Ms. Colman looked sort of excited, so I had a feeling it was a good and special announcement.

I glanced at Ricky Torres next to me. We grinned at each other.

"My announcement," said Ms. Colman, when my friends and I were quiet, "is that our class is going to give all the people at Stoneybrook Manor a special Grandparents' Day."

"Goody," I said.

Ms. Colman smiled. Then she went on. "Grandparents' Day can be whatever we make it. I thought we could put on a program, and make a gift for every person staying at the manor."

I raised my hand. "What kind of program would we put on?" I asked, when Ms. Colman called on me.

"Whatever you want. Some variety might be nice. Maybe a skit, some songs, some poetry. I think you should break into groups. Then each group can plan one part of the program. The important thing is that everyone in this class must join in on Grandparents' Day. If you are shy about being in the program, you do not have to sing or act. But you must still help make presents, and come to Stoneybrook Manor to pass them out, and to say hello to the people there. This is a class project."

"Will we be graded?" asked Nancy from the back of the room. She did not even bother to raise her hand. And she sounded scared to death.

"Graded?" repeated Ms. Colman. "No. But you must be part of the project."

I turned around to peek at Nancy. She looked just as scared as she sounded.

"So," said Ms. Colman, "please think about what we could do in our program, whether you'd like to be in the program, and what kinds of gifts we could make. Remember that we have to make a lot of them."

"Oh, boy," I whispered to Ricky. "I can't wait to be in the program."

"Maybe we could put on a play about super heroes," Ricky whispered back. "I would like to be Super Ricky and carry a sword."

"I just want to be the star of some play," I said.

When school was over I ran to Nancy. "Here is your chance to act," I told her. "You can be an actress. You can be in a play on Grandparents' Day. I want to be the star, though."

I expected Nancy to say, "No, I want to be the star."

That is the way Nancy and I are when it comes to acting.

Instead, Nancy's eyes filled with tears.

"No," she said. "I am not going to Stoneybrook Manor. No one can make me go there. I will not visit all those old people."

34

"But this is a class project," I reminded her.

"I don't care. I'm not going in that place."

"Not even to meet Grandma B?"

"Not even to meet Grandma B. I guess I will just have to be sick on Grandparents' Day."

I did not say anything. I knew Nancy would never do that.

Big News

After a few more visits to Grandma B, I discovered something. I discovered I was getting tired of Grandma B. I know that is not a nice thing to say, but it was true.

Why was I getting tired of Grandma B? Because here are the things she always wanted to do:

— make me listen to funny, old music, the kind with lots of violins in it.

— teach me how to do old-time dances like the waltz. Some of them had weird names, such as the foxtrot.

— look through her photo albums with her.

"Karen," Grandma B would say, "you must learn how to do these things." (She meant the dancing.) "And everyone should appreciate classical music. How else will you become cultured?"

I wasn't sure what "cultured" meant. I did remember that once when I was sick with a strep throat, the doctor took a throat culture, but I did not think that had anything to do with what Grandma B was talking about.

Anyway, I did not like the violin music. I like radio music with rhythm and lots of drums beating — and words to it.

What I wanted to do at the manor was go to arts and crafts with Grandma B. Or read stories with her. Or better yet, *make up* stories.

So I was just a little tired of visiting my newest grandma.

I guess that's why I skipped one visit to the manor.

This is what happened:

It was a Wednesday evening. The phone rang at the little house.

"I'll get it!" I yelled.

"Indoor voice," Seth reminded me.

"Sorry," I told him. Then I picked up the phone. "Hello?" I said.

"Hi, Karen. It's me, Kristy."

"Hi, Kristy!"

"Listen, I'm calling a Krushers practice for tomorrow," she said. "Can you come?"

I thought for a moment. I was supposed to go to the manor and visit Grandma B the next day. But I really didn't want to listen to any more violin music. And I was tired of waltzing and doing the foxtrot.

"Sure," I said to Kristy. "I can come."

"Great! Thanks, Karen. See you tomorrow."

I hung up the phone. I knew I would have to tell Mommy what I had done. I thought Mommy might be mad, but all she said was, "You'll have to call Grandma B and tell her you can't visit her."

"Okay," I replied.

That would not be easy. But I did it. I said, "I'm really sorry, but I have to practice with my softball team tomorrow."

Grandma B sounded disappointed when I told her that. But she did say, "Good luck, Karen! Play well."

Maybe Grandma B brought me good luck. I did play well the next day. So did Andrew. He's on the team, too. We both hit the ball

a couple of times. Andrew even got a home run!

Mommy picked us up after practice. She drove us back to the little house. (Andrew talked about his home run all the way.)

When we reached our house, I saw Nancy. She was in her front yard. As soon as *she* saw *us*, she ran to meet our car. She was waving something in the air.

"Hi, Nancy," I said as I got out of the car.

"Hi! Guess what! Big news!" Nancy replied in a rush.

Big Mama

"**B**ig news?" I repeated. "What is it?"

I climbed out of our car.

"It's this!" exclaimed Nancy, waving the something in the air again. "Come on, Karen. Let's go up to your room."

I ran into our house and up to my room. Nancy followed me. We plopped down on my bed together.

"Okay," I said. "*Now* tell me your big news. And what is *that*?" I pointed to the something. It was an envelope. Another fat one.

"This," began Nancy proudly, "is a letter from your grandmother in Nebraska. From *my* new pen-pal grandma!"

"You mean you wrote to her and she wrote back?" I asked.

"Yup," said Nancy.

Hmm. Granny hadn't answered *my* letter yet.

"And this isn't all she sent," Nancy went on. "She sent me a pair of mittens with my name on them. She knitted them herself."

"Really?"

Boy.

I couldn't believe it. Well, that just wasn't fair at all. Granny knitted me a pair of mittens with my name on them last year. I had thought that my Karen-mittens were very special. But I guess not. I guess Granny knits name-mittens for any girl who comes along.

"You want to see what's in the letter?" Nancy asked me.

"Sure," I replied, even though I did not care much.

"Okay," said Nancy. "Well, the letter is three pages long. And your grandma sent more pictures! Here is one of the barn cat and her kittens. There are five kittens. And two of them look like Pearl. Pearl is the barn cat."

"I know who Pearl is," I said crossly.

Nancy did not notice that I was cross. She went on talking. "And here is a picture of your grandfather's new plow. And this is the new decoration on the front door of

44

your grandparents' house. And this is Spinky the horse.

"Karen?" Nancy said.

"Yeah?"

"In her letter, your grandmother said I should decide what to call her. I started *my* letter to her, 'Dear Pen-Pal Grandma,' but she thinks that name is too long. So I thought and thought. I can't call her Mrs. Engle. Not if she's sort of my grandmother. And I can't call her Granny, because that's what you and Andrew call her. So I thought of a new name. I am going to call her Big Mama. Do you think she will like it?"

I was not sure. I thought Granny might *not* like it. But I did not tell Nancy that. I was just a little mad at Nancy. I was mad because Granny had knitted name-mittens for her, and sent her more letters than she had sent me.

So I said to Nancy, "Big Mama. Let me see. Yes, I think that is a perfect name for Granny. Start your next letter, 'Dear Big Mama,' and see what happens."

"Okay!" said Nancy. She was smiling.

"Do you want to play with Emily Junior?" I asked. I stood up to open my rat's cage.

"No," replied Nancy. "I mean, no thank you. I am very busy. I better go now. I have to write to Big Mama. Also, I have decided to make a present for her, since she knitted mittens for me. I wonder what I should make for her."

"I don't know," I said. "But tell me what happens when you get a letter back from . . . Big Mama."

"I will!" cried Nancy. She ran out of my room and was gone.

Necklaces and
Pencil Cups

"Class! May I have your attention, please? It's time to put your books away."

Ms. Colman was trying to get our attention. It was a Friday afternoon, and we were hard at work. What did she want? I wondered. School was not over yet. Maybe she was going to make another Surprising Announcement.

When we were sitting quietly at our desks, Ms. Colman said, "Today, class, we will start talking about our program for Grandparents' Day. It is time to begin planning it. We have a lot of work to do."

I glanced back at Nancy. She looked very nervous again.

"I want to do two things," Ms. Colman went on. "I want you to decide what gifts to make for the people at Stoneybrook Manor. And if you are going to be in the program, I want you to break into groups and decide what you'd like to do. Each group should plan something different."

Oh, boy! This was getting exciting! Grandma B and everyone were going to love Grandparents' Day.

"Who has an idea for gifts that we could make?" asked Ms. Colman.

Natalie Springer's hand shot up.

"Yes, Natalie?"

"How about pot holders?"

"Well, that is a nice thought, but the people at the manor do not have to cook. They eat in a dining room. Any other ideas?"

This time Ricky raised his hand.

"Cakes and cookies," he suggested.

"Another good idea," said Ms. Colman. "But a lot of the people at the manor are on special diets. Some of them cannot eat cakes and cookies."

After lots of talking, we decided to make necklaces for the women and pencil cups for the men. We would make the necklaces by stringing painted macaroni onto yarn. We would make the pencil cups by gluing wrapping paper around soup cans.

"Good ideas," said Ms. Colman. "Everybody, please remember to save soup cans and bring them in from home. Macaroni, too. Now you may break into groups of three or four, if you want to be in the program."

I wanted to be in the program, of course. So did Hannie. So did Nancy, even though she is afraid of old people. She just could not pass up a chance to act in front of an audience. Guess who else joined our group. Ricky Torres!

"How come you want to work with girls?" Hannie asked him.

"Because I know you are going to put on a play," he replied. "And I want to be in it. I want to be Super Ricky. I want to carry a sword."

"But Ricky, we have not decided to put on a play about super heroes," I told him.

"I think it's a good idea," spoke up Nancy. "I could be Super Nancy, and you guys could be Super Karen, Super Hannie, and Super Ricky."

"Is that what we want to do? A super heroes play?" I asked.

"*I* want to put on a play about a little lost kitten," said Hannie.

"Oh, that is so lame. That is girl stuff," said Ricky.

"But I *am* a girl!"

"So what?"

In the end, we decided that we would have to think about our play some more. Whatever we did, I wanted it to be the best part of the whole program.

Paddington Bear

I missed another visit to Grandma B.

It wasn't my fault, though. I had an earache.

When I called Grandma B to tell her I could not see her the next day, she said, "Feel better soon, Karen. Do everything your mother tells you to do."

I knew she was a little disappointed, though. She also said, "I hope you will be able to come next time. I miss you."

And I missed Grandma B.

Sort of.

* * *

By Tuesday, my earache was all gone. I was back in school. So that afternoon, I rode the bus to Stoneybrook Manor again. Grandma B was waiting for me at the door.

"Hello, hello!" she cried. She kissed my cheek. She smelled like cherry candy.

I kissed Grandma B. I discovered that I *had* missed her. But I certainly hoped that she was not going to try to give me any more culture. That was boring.

"Let's go to my room, Karen," said Grandma B.

Uh-oh. I could almost hear the violin music.

But when we reached Grandma B's room, she did not turn on the record player. Instead, she sat down on her bed. I sat next to her.

"Karen," said Grandma B, looking solemn, "it is almost time for the High Holy Days."

The holidays? Not really, I thought. Christmas was more than two months away.

Well, maybe to some people two or three months did not seem like much time. But it seemed like forever to me.

"I take the High Holy Days very seriously," Grandma B went on.

"Oh, me, too," I replied. I just adore Christmas. It is the best time of year. I like Santa Claus and presents and decorating trees. I like school vacation and eating turkey and singing Christmas carols.

"Well, I'm glad to hear that," said Grandma B. She smiled. "I have always observed the Ten Days of Penitence."

The Ten Days of Penitence? Did Grandma B mean the Twelve Days of Christmas? I wasn't sure. Maybe there was something about Christmas that I did not know. After all, my two families do not go to church very often. But I did not want to admit that to Grandma B. The holidays seemed so important to her. So I nodded my head and pretended I knew what she was talking about.

Grandma B went on. She talked about

Rosh Hashanah and Yom Kippur and a lot of other stuff I'd never heard of before. I did not pay much attention. And after awhile, I was very bored. I waited until Grandma B came to a stopping place. Then I reached into my backpack. I pulled out a copy of *Paddington Marches On.* I love Paddington Bear. I am trying to read all of the books about him.

"Grandma B?" I said. "Do you know who Paddington Bear is?"

"No," she replied. "I don't believe I do."

"Well, this is Paddington," I told her. I showed her the book. "He is a very special bear. He lives in England with a nice family. But he came from Darkest Peru. And he can talk. The Brown family doesn't think that is strange at all. Do you want to read to me? You can read five pages, and then we will switch and I will read five pages to you."

"All right," said Grandma B. She began to read.

We spent the rest of the hour laughing

about Paddington. I was glad that Grandma B liked him as much as I do. Still, I had to admit two things to myself. 1. I was relieved when we stopped talking about high holidays. 2. No matter what, I was still looking forward to Grandparents' Day.

Adopted Grandchildren

It was a Friday, but it was a special one. It was a going-to-Daddy's Friday. Late that afternoon, just before dinner, Mommy would drive Andrew and me to the big house for the weekend.

That made Friday pretty special. But something else made it even more special. In the mail that day I received a letter from Granny in the state of Nebraska.

"Oh, boy!" I cried.

I took the letter and ran to my room.

I needed some privacy.

"Dear Karen," Granny's letter began, "I am so happy to have you as my granddaughter and Nancy as my pen-pal granddaughter." (I am really only her stepgranddaughter, I thought.) "Guess what," the letter went on. "Nancy calls me Big Mama now. Isn't that funny? I just love the name."

Hmm. Granny *liked* the name "Big Mama"? I had not expected that.

Granny's letter was two pages long. She told me about the new tractor and a bunch of stuff I already knew from Nancy's letters.

She did not send me any pictures. But she told me she liked the things that Nancy had been sending her.

I had not expected Granny to like Nancy so much. Granny sounded as if she liked Nancy as much as she liked me. Was that because I was just Granny's stepgranddaughter? I wondered. And what about adopted grandchildren? How did grandmas feel about them?

There was only one person to ask. Nannie. She was the only grandma I knew who had a really-and-truly adopted grandchild. And that was Emily Michelle, my adopted sister.

At the big house that night I had a talk with Nannie. I waited until after dinner, when the house was quiet. Daddy and Elizabeth were reading. Sam and Charlie had gone to a dance at the high school. Kristy was baby-sitting across the street at Hannie's house. And David Michael, Andrew, and Emily were upstairs in the playroom.

"Nannie?" I said.

Nannie was in the den. She was watching TV and knitting. She was knitting a sweater for me! I had helped her choose the colors.

"Yes?" said Nannie.

"You have lots of grandchildren," I told her. "You have Kristy and David Michael and Sam and Charlie, who are your regular grandchildren. And you have Andrew and

me. We are your stepgrandchildren. And
Emily is your adopted grandchild."

"That's right," said Nannie. "And I love
you all."

"Just the same?" I asked.

"I love you the same amount, but for
different reasons. And the reasons don't
have anything to do with whether you're
steps or adopted or 'regular' kids. Grand-

mothers have room in their lives for lots of different kinds of grandchildren."

I sighed gratefully. "Thank you, Nannie," I said. I kissed her.

I felt much, much better.

Goblins and Ghosts

On Saturday morning, the doorbell rang.

"I'll get it!" I said. (I remembered to use my indoor voice.)

I ran to the front door of the big house. "Who is it?" I called.

"It's me, Hannie," said Hannie.

I let Hannie inside.

"Hi!" I said. "I have a great idea. Let's work on our play for Grandparents' Day. Wouldn't it be great if we went to school on Monday, and we had a terrific play for our group?"

"Sure!" exclaimed Hannie.

"Come on up to my room, then," I said.

Hannie and I clattered upstairs. We sat on the floor in my room.

"I have been thinking," I told Hannie. "The people at the manor might not understand a play about super heroes. But Halloween is coming up, and *every*one knows about Halloween. So let's put on a scary play."

"Okay," agreed Hannie. (Hannie usually agrees with me.)

"Now what kind of scary play should we put on? Who will the play be about?"

"Morbidda Destiny?" suggested Hannie.

Morbidda Destiny is the name I gave to the weird old woman who lives next door to Daddy. I know she is a witch.

"Or how about a play about a *ghost* and a witch? We could write one about Ben Brewer and Morbidda Destiny." (I am pretty sure that the third floor of Daddy's house is haunted by a ghost named Ben Brewer.)

"Or maybe," said Hannie, "we could put

64

on a play about Georgie the Ghost. You
know, the ghost in the books?"

"Yes!" I cried. "I could be Georgie, the
shy ghost. And you could be his friend Miss
Oliver the Owl. And Ricky could be his
friend Herman the Cat. And Nancy could
be Mrs. Whittaker." (Georgie lives in the
Whittakers' attic.)

"But who would be *Mr.* Whittaker?" asked
Hannie.

"Oh. Hmm. I don't know. I guess we

don't have enough people for a play about Georgie."

"How about Ghostbusters?" asked Hannie.

"Would your adopted grandma know who the Ghostbusters are?" I asked.

Hannie shook her head.

"Neither would Grandma B," I told her.

We went back to thinking. But we did not get any good ideas.

Some One Came Knocking

"I need more yarn!"

"Can someone please pass the glue?"

"Ew! I have red paint all over my fingers!"

On Monday afternoon Ms. Colman's class was hard at work. We were making the macaroni necklaces and the pencil cups.

Here is what you have to do to make necklaces: Take some macaroni. (Not cooked, because it would be slimy.) Paint the macaroni pretty colors. You can even put polka dots on it. Then string the macaroni onto a long piece of yarn, tie the yarn in a knot, and you have a beautiful necklace!

To make a pencil cup, take an empty soup can. Make sure it is washed very well and that there are no sharp edges. Then cut out a piece of wrapping paper, spread glue on the wrong side, and wrap it around the can. That is all you have to do. Isn't that easy?

Hannie, Nancy, Ricky, and I were sitting together. We had pushed our desks into one big square. We were making the neck-

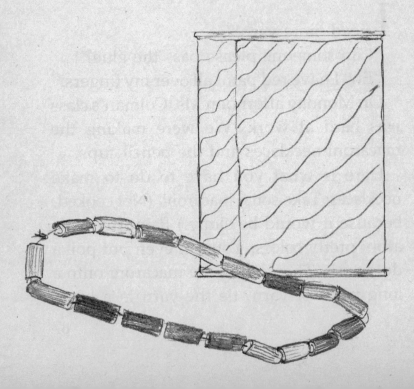

laces and pencil cups. And we were talking about our play.

"Hannie and I thought we could put on a play about Georgie the shy little ghost," I said. "But we need more people."

"You know what?" said Ricky. "On Saturday I got a book of poems. Some of the poems are really funny. I think we should recite poems."

"Nooo," I groaned. "I want to put on a scary play."

"So do I," said Nancy. (She wanted to be the star.)

"Well," said Ricky, "some of the poems are scary. We could recite scary poems."

"I like that idea," said Hannie. "I wanted to be in a play, but reciting poems would be fun."

"I guess that idea is okay," said Nancy. "Karen?"

"Maybe," I answered. "Ricky, what scary poems do you know?"

"Well," said Ricky. "There's a poem in my book called 'Some One.' I think it is scary. It is about a person who hears a knock at his door, but when he opens the door, nobody is there."

"Ooh," I said.

"I know a scary poem, too," said Nancy. "It's about a tree . . . a *strange* tree. One that is all twisted and it looks at you."

"Ew," said Hannie.

"Hey! I just thought of a poem that is funny *and* scary," I cried. "It's about a little boy whose name is James James Morrison Morrison Weatherby George Dupree. He is supposed to baby-sit for his mother, only one day his mother says she is going downtown by herself, and after that she is never heard from again. Isn't that weird?"

"Yes," said Ricky. "Extra weird. Hannie, do you know any scary poems?"

"Let me think," she replied. After a long time, she said, "Last year in first grade I wrote a poem about Halloween."

"Wait a second," I interrupted her. "Is this the one that begins, 'Black cat with a tall black hat'?"

"Yes," said Hannie.

"Let's stick to grown-ups' poems," I said.

Hannie looked grumpy. But she agreed that we should all try to find scary poems, especially poems about Halloween. Then we would choose several to memorize for the Grandparents' Day program.

I could hardly wait to go poem-hunting.

Young and Old

D*ing-dong.*

"Someone's at the door!" yelled Andrew.

"Andrew, use your indoor voice," I told him. "You don't have to shout. You're sitting in my lap."

Andrew and I were at home with Mommy. I was looking at a book of poems. I was hunting for scary poems, or poems about Halloween. This took a long time. Andrew wanted me to read every poem to him.

Then the doorbell rang.

"I'll get it," I said. "Andrew, I'll read

more to you later." I stood up, and Andrew fell out of my lap. "Sorry!" I called as I ran for the door.

Nancy was standing on our front steps. She was holding a letter, but she had a funny look on her face.

Not another letter from Granny in the state of Nebraska, I thought.

"I got a letter from Big Mama," Nancy told me, as she came indoors.

I sighed. "Another one?" I said.

"Yes. But this one is different. Big Mama sent more pictures — see? They are of herself and — and Big Daddy. I guess that is what I should call your grandfather." Nancy still had that funny look on her face. Now I knew why.

"What did you think of the photos?" I asked.

Nancy and I had reached my bedroom. We sat on the floor and let Emily Junior out of her cage.

"Well," said Nancy. "It's funny. Big Mama sounds so *young* in her letters. She talks

about taking care of the animals and working on the farm. But she looks old in the pictures. Her hair is almost white. And her face has wrinkles. Your grandfather looks old, too."

"But see? That's just what I've been trying to tell you," I said. "Looking old does not mean acting old. Lots of grandparents look old but do not act old. And some do not even look old, like Nannie."

"I know," said Nancy.

"Then there is my Grandma Packett. She is Mommy's mother. She looks old but does not act old. Same with Grandma B."

"Tell me about Grandma B," said Nancy.

"Okay." (Nancy had hardly asked anything about my adopted grandmother.) "Grandma B," I began, "looks pretty old."

"As old as Big Mama?" asked Nancy.

"Yes," I replied. "But she likes to sing and dance."

"Dance?" exclaimed Nancy. She looked very surprised. "I guess that means she does not need a wheelchair. Does she need a cane?"

"No. She walks all by herself. And you know what one of the nurses at the manor told me?"

"What?" asked Nancy.

"She told me that Grandma B talks on the phone every evening — just like a teenager! I think she talks to her children and grandchildren."

"Maybe," said Nancy slowly, "Grandparents' Day won't be so bad after all. I do not think I will mind meeting Mrs. Barnard. I will probably be afraid of the really old people. But Mrs. Barnard will be okay, since she's like Big Mama.''

I smiled. I wanted Nancy to like Grandparents' Day. I wanted her to like Grandma B. Maybe Nancy and Grandma B would even become friends. I did not want to be Grandma B's only kid friend. I was getting pretty tired of dancing and of violin music. And I had decided that four grandmas were enough. I did not need to set a grandmother record.

Some One Strange
Came Knocking

On a Thursday afternoon, Ms. Colman made one of her announcements.

"Tomorrow," she said, "we will hold a dress rehearsal for your Grandparents' Day program. Does everyone know what a dress rehearsal is?"

"No!" yelled Ricky and Natalie and some other kids.

"Okay," said Ms. Colman. "A dress rehearsal is a rehearsal when you dress in your costumes and you use your props. You put on the entire program from beginning to end without stopping, even if you make mistakes. So come in tomorrow with everything you need if you have a part in the program. Oh, and another thing. No more reading from scripts. You should have your plays and poems and songs memorized by now."

Boy, Ms. Colman's announcement surprised me.

"Ricky?" I said after school. "Hannie? Nancy? Are we ready for a dress rehearsal tomorrow?"

"I guess so," replied Nancy.

"We don't have costumes," Ricky pointed out.

"I know," I said. "But we haven't memorized our poems yet. Well, I guess we'll just have to work hard tonight. See you tomorrow, you guys!"

Early the next afternoon, our dress rehearsal began. The first part of the program was a song about pumpkins. Natalie and

Jannie sang it. They were wearing their pumpkin Halloween costumes from last year. They started to sing, *"The pumpkin ran away, before Thanksgiving Day!"* But Jannie's pumpkin suit kept slipping down, and she began to laugh. She couldn't stop. Natalie had to finish the song herself.

Then a bunch of boys put on a play they had written. It was about a rocket ship blasting off, and astronauts finding dinosaurs on the moon. The boys had forgotten to bring in their dinosaurs, though. They used chalkboard erasers and lunchboxes instead. The play did not make much sense. They would say things like "Look! There is a diplodocus!" as they pointed to a Teen-age Mutant Ninja Turtles lunchbox.

I tried so hard not to laugh that my face turned red and I snorted.

Then it was our turn.

Ricky, Hannie, Nancy, and I stood in front of the classroom. We were each going to recite two short poems.

Ricky went first. He was going to recite "Some One" and "Strange Trees." At first Nancy was going to recite "Strange Trees," but then she found two other poems she wanted to recite, so Ricky said he would recite "Strange Trees." He just decided to do that two days ago.

I guess he didn't know "Strange Trees" very well. He got his poems all mixed up. Instead of saying, "Some one came knocking/At my wee, small door," he said, "Some one *strange* came knocking/At my wee, small door." And the end of his poem was more mixed up than the beginning. He said, "So I know not who had yellow wrinkles/At all, at all, at all."

Everyone laughed. Even Hannie and Nancy and I. But we did not recite our own poems much better. I called James James Morrison Morrison Weatherby George Dupree, "John Jacob Jingleheimer Weatherby George Duschmidt."

When the dress rehearsal was over, Ms. Colman sighed loudly.

"Class," she began, "our program must be in much better shape before we put it on for the people at the manor. Your homework tonight is to practice. We will hold another dress rehearsal on Monday."

Ready, Set, Go

"Mommy! Mommy! Today is Grandparents' Day!" I cried.

I had just woken up. Grandparents' Day was the first thing I thought of.

Mommy poked her head into my room.

"Good morning," she said. "Are you excited?"

"I am *very* excited," I told her. "I think I am ready, too. I know both of my poems. Listen to this. 'James James/Morrison Morrison/Weatherby George Dupree/Took great/Care of his mother/Though he was only

83

three.' I know the rest, too," I said to Mommy.

"That's wonderful!" she exclaimed.

"And my clothes are laid out," I went on. I pointed to the chair in my room. The night before, I had chosen my red-and-white-striped dress, red tights, and my very special black patent leather shoes.

"Is it okay to wear my party shoes to school?" I asked Mommy.

"Yes," she replied. "Today is a special occasion."

Ooh. I just love special occasions.

In school that afternoon, we held one last dress rehearsal. Everybody looked terrific. Jannie's pumpkin costume had been fixed. It did not slip down anymore. Hannie and Nancy were as dressed up as I was. And Ricky was wearing a suit with a bow tie. We looked like we were ready to have our school pictures taken.

The last rehearsal went well. Jannie and Natalie sang, *"The pumpkin ran away, before*

Thanksgiving Day! Said he, 'You'll make a pie of me if I should stay!' "

Then Ricky recited "Some One" and "Strange Trees." He did not mix them up at all. I recited "Disobedience." (That is the poem about James James Morrison Morrison Weatherby George Dupree.) And I recited a poem I had made up. It was about a girl who lived in a house haunted by a ghost, with a witch next door. It was much better than Hannie's first-grade poem about the black cat with the tall black hat. And Hannie and Nancy recited their poems.

When our group was finished Ms. Colman applauded!

Soon school was over. At last, at last, at last it was time to go to Stoneybrook Manor. We gathered up all of our things — our props and costumes and, of course, the boxes of pencil cups and macaroni necklaces. We climbed on a yellow bus that was waiting in front of school.

Hannie and Nancy and I squeezed onto

one seat. We needed to be together. Hannie
and I were gigundo excited.

But Nancy was gigundo scared.

"I do not want to go to the manor. Why
do we have to go there?" she kept saying.
She gazed out the window.

"We are going to make the people at the
manor so, so happy," I said.

"Yeah," agreed Hannie. "They will like
their presents. And they will *love* our program. I just know they will."

"Can't they love everything without me?" muttered Nancy.

"Oh, Nancy," I said.

The next thing we knew, the bus had arrived at the manor. The driver parked in a lot in back of the building. My friends and I climbed out of the bus.

"Don't Be Scared!"

Ms. Colman led our class to the front doors of Stoneybrook Manor. The room mothers had come along again for the trip. They helped us carry the boxes of presents.

At the front door, Mrs. Fellows greeted us.

"Hello!" she said. She smiled a lot. She seemed very jolly. "Welcome. For all you newcomers, my name is Mrs. Fellows. Thank you for coming. We have all been looking forward to Grandparents' Day. Follow me. I will take you to the all-purpose room."

I already knew how to get to the all-purpose room. I knew my way around Stoneybrook Manor very well. But I followed Mrs. Fellows, along with my class. And when I reached the room, I was surprised.

I saw lots of new faces. I guess they were people who did not leave their rooms much. Some of them looked very, very, very, *very* old. Some looked sick. For the first time, I felt a little afraid. But then I looked at Nancy. I thought she was going to faint.

I grabbed her hand. "Don't be scared!" I whispered loudly. "They are all glad we came."

"But that lady over there is asleep in her wheelchair," Nancy whispered back.

"Well, everyone else is glad we came," I replied. "They really are. A lot of them are like Grandma B. They do not have any family nearby."

I saw Grandma B then and waved to her. She grinned and waved back.

I was just about to take Nancy to her

when Ms. Colman gathered our class together. We stood in front of those old, old faces.

"Girls and boys," said Ms. Colman, "we will put on the program first. Then we will hand out the presents. So please get ready to perform."

My friends and I took off our jackets. We got our props ready. Some kids fixed up their costumes.

At last Ms. Colman said to our audience, "Our program is about to begin. We have worked very hard on it. I hope you will have fun watching it. I now present the second grade from Stoneybrook Academy."

Oooh. My heart was beating fast. I had stage fright. I held onto Hannie and Nancy. We watched Natalie and Jannie sing the pumpkin song. They did very well, and everybody clapped for them.

Then the boys put on their space-and-dinosaur play. This time, they were ready with their props.

"Look! There is a diplodocus!" exclaimed

Hank Reubens. He pointed to a plastic dinosaur. "And there is a triceratops. We have found dinosaurs on the moon. We are heroes!"

The boys all said, "The end," and took a bow.

More applause.

Now it was *our* turn. Ricky went first. I went second. Nancy went third. Hannie went fourth. Do you know what? *We did not make one single mistake.*

Everyone clapped and Grandma B put her fingers in her mouth and whistled. "Yea, Karen!" she cried.

The program was over. And the people at the manor had a surprise for *us*. They served punch and cookies. Yummy-yummers! Then my friends and I began to pass out the gifts. Nancy and I were heading toward Grandma B with a nice macaroni necklace when Ms. Colman said, "Karen? Nancy? Would you come here, please?"

The High Holy Days

Uh-oh, I thought. Are we in trouble? I tried to think of something I had done wrong. Had I used my outdoor voice? Had I spilled punch?

Nancy and I turned around and walked to Ms. Colman.

"Girls," she said seriously, "there are six residents of the manor who could not come to the program. They are not feeling well and they have to stay in their beds. But we want to give them gifts, too. I thought it would be nice if they got them from us, and not from a nurse or from Mrs. Fellows later. They would like to see two young faces. So would you please go with Mrs. Fellows to hand out the gifts? Here are four pencil cups and two necklaces."

I gulped. I looked at Nancy. She would not want to do this. But you have to pay attention to your teacher. So I said, "Okay," to Ms. Colman. Nancy could not speak. She just nodded her head.

"Good girls. Thank you," said Ms. Colman.

Nancy and I followed Mrs. Fellows through the hallways. Nancy held onto my hand so tightly I thought she would break it.

The old people were really nice, though. They loved their gifts. One man looked like he was two hundred years old. He could not talk. But when I said, "I am Karen and this is Nancy, and we have a present for you," he smiled. He did not have any teeth, but Nancy did not mind. She liked his smile anyway.

When we had given away all the gifts,

Nancy was still looking happy. Mrs. Fellows took us back to the all-purpose room.

"*Now*," I said to Nancy, "come meet Grandma B."

Grandma B was sitting on a couch. She was wearing a macaroni necklace.

"Hi!" I exclaimed. "Grandma B, this is my friend Nancy. Nancy Dawes. She does not have any grandmas or grandpas. Except for a pen-pal grandma."

"Hello, Nancy Dawes. How are you?"

"I'm fine," said Nancy shyly. "How are you?"

"Just fine. I am very excited. I am getting ready for the High Holy Days."

"Really?" said Nancy. "Me, too! . . . Wait a second. I thought Karen said your family lives in Chicago. Are you going to Chicago for Rosh Hashanah and Yom Kippur? Are you staying for Succot?"

"No," said Grandma B. She looked a little sad. "But we observe the holidays at the manor. And Mrs. Fellows will probably drive me to temple."

Oh, I thought. High *Holy* Days. Not the holidays. Not Christmas. Nancy celebrates different holidays than I do. She is Jewish. I guessed Grandma B was, too.

"But," Nancy was saying, "you can't go to temple alone. You need a family. Why don't you come to our synagogue with us? And then maybe you could come home to our house. Mommy always makes challah and honey cake and — and everything!"

I could not believe Nancy was so excited

talking to an old person. Grandma B seemed excited, too.

"Do you like to dance?" she asked Nancy.

"Oh, yes!" Nancy replied. "I am going to be an actress one day. I have to learn to sing and dance and maybe play the piano."

"Do you like to listen to music?" asked Grandma B.

"Yes," said Nancy again. "Mommy and Daddy play very beautiful music on our stereo. They say it is classical."

I left Grandma B and Nancy talking about music and acting. They looked comfortable and happy, sitting together on the couch.

Nancy's Grandmothers

Well, you will never guess what. I have just my four regular grandmothers again — Granny, Grandma, Nannie, and Neena. And now Nancy has an adopted grandma. Her grandma is Grandma B.

Grandma B went to the synagogue with the Daweses at Rosh Hashanah, Yom Kippur, and Succot. I am not sure what happens on those holy days. But they are very important to Nancy and her parents and Grandma B.

Mr. and Mrs. Dawes only minded a little

that Nancy had invited Grandma B to join them on the holy days. I mean, they didn't mind that Grandma B was coming. They thought that was nice. But they minded that Nancy had invited Grandma B without asking them first if she could do that.

I have the same rule at my house. *First* I have to ask Mommy or Seth if I can invite someone over. *Then* I do the inviting.

Anyway, the Daweses and Grandma B like each other very much. Grandma B spends a lot of time at Nancy's house now. I found out that Succot is a special Thanksgiving festival. Also, Grandma B brings her favorite violin music over to Nancy's house and they all listen to it. Nancy *likes* the violin music.

Grandma B taught Nancy to waltz.

Here is some more news. One day I was watching TV. I saw a girl doing fancy tricks on a balance beam, and turning cartwheels and flipping hands to feet, hands to feet.

"She is a gymnast," Mommy told me.

"Can I be a gymnast?" I asked.

"If you take gymnastics," replied Mommy. "Do you want to take lessons?"

"Yes!" I said.

So Mommy signed me up for lessons at the Y.

Here is the bad thing: The lessons were held on the days I was supposed to go to Stoneybrook Manor.

Here is the good thing: *Nancy* wanted to adopt Grandma B. So she did! Now Nancy goes to the manor two times a week. She is not afraid of the old people there. Well, she is a *little* afraid of the ones in wheelchairs. But that is all.

And she has two grandmas now — a penpal grandma and an adopted grandma. They are not the *kinds* of grandmas most people have, but at least she has two of them. And Grandma B has a family in Stoneybrook. Nancy said she has already invited Grandma B over for Hanukkah and for Passover Seder.

Me? I've got my four grandmas back. That's all I need. I did not *really* have to set a grandmother record.

Here are some of the things I am learning in gymnastics: cartwheels, backward somersaults, shoulder rolls, and round-offs.

One day after school I was in the backyard at Mommy's. I was practicing my gymnastics.

"Watch me, Andrew!" I cried.

I turned a cartwheel.

I landed on my bottom.

"Was that supposed to happen?" asked Andrew.

"No," I replied. I would have to practice some more. I did not mind. I *love* gymnastics.

"Karen!" Mommy called from the back door. "Phone for you. It's Granny."

Goody, goody, goody! Granny in the state of Nebraska.

I ran inside. I could not wait to speak to my own special grandma.

About the Author

ANN M. MARTIN lives in New York City and loves animals. Her cat, Mouse, knows how to take the phone off the hook.

Other books by Ann M. Martin that you might enjoy are *Stage Fright, Me and Katie (the Pest)*, and the books in *The Baby-sitters Club* series.

Ann likes ice cream, the beach, and *I Love Lucy*. And she has her own little sister, whose name is Jane.

Little Sister

Don't miss #11

KAREN'S PRIZE

"Please answer your brother's question," said Seth.

"A spelling bee is when everyone lines up and gets to spell words," I said.

"Which words?" asked Andrew.

"The words on the list the teacher gives you. But that doesn't matter. All that matters is that I'm going to be the best junior speller in the state of Connecticut. C-O-N-N-E-C-T-I-C-U-T! You know what a state is, don't you?"

"Nope," said Andrew.

"I can't believe it! You don't know anything!" I said.

"I do too know things. I know you're a sore winner!" said Andrew.

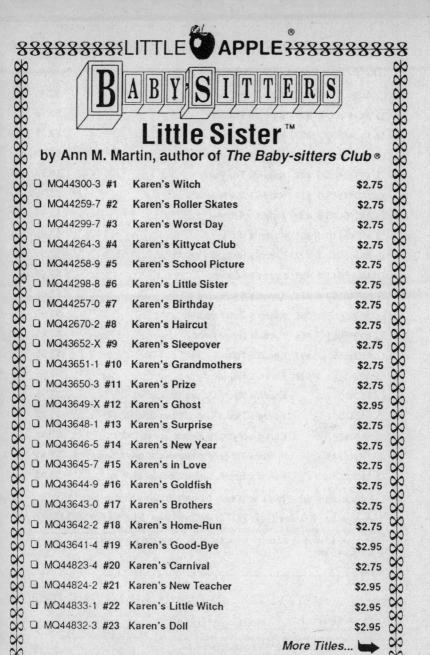

LITTLE 🍎 APPLE ®

BABY-SITTERS
Little Sister™
by Ann M. Martin, author of *The Baby-sitters Club* ®

More Titles... ➡